MW00892587

do not open the door!

written by christopher bell
illustrated by oliver bundoc

ISBN-13: 978-0692303399
ISBN-10: 0692303391

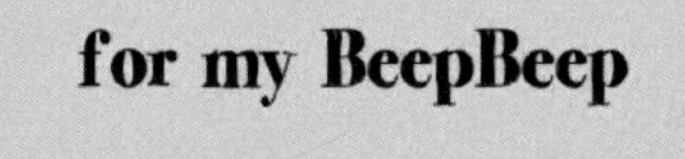
for my BeepBeep

this is a story about three siblings.
siblings are people who
have the same parents.
Like brothers.
or sisters.

or two sisters and one brother.

the oldest was a sister.
she liked to pretend she
was big and mean, but
she was really very nice,
once you got to know her.
she tried to hide this
by wearing lots of black.

her name was kelly.

the middle was also a sister.
she liked to pretend she was
small and nice, but she was
really very small and very,
very nice, once you
got to know her.
there was no way to hide this.

her name was harmony.

the youngest was a brother.
he didn't like to pretend.
he was very, very big and
had a hard time making
good choices. Still, he was
a sweet boy (most of the time)
once you got to know him,
even when he was making
not so great choices.

his name was simon.

they liked being siblings very much.

there is somebody at the door.
do not open the door!
knock! knock!

it could be a MONSTER!
a monster?
you always think everything could be a monster.

but it could be!
it could be a monster with...

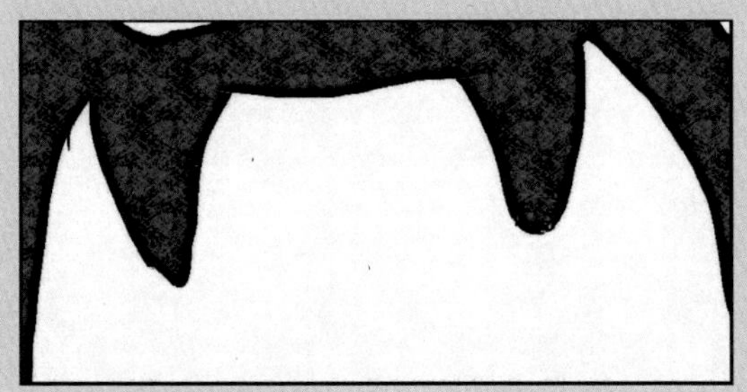

big, sharp teeth...

and three eyeballs...

and razor claws...

and giant horns!

i do not want to see a monster with big, sharp teeth and three eyeballs and razor claws and giant horns!
i do not want to see that either!

and what if he comes in here and stuffs us all in a sack?!
i do not want to be stuffed in a sack!

he might take us away to his monster house and tell us to make him waffles, and when we make him waffles, he might tell us he does not even like waffles!
i like waffles!

and instead of waffles,
he might eat my face!
i like my face!

it is not a monster.
i am opening the door.
no!
DO NOT OPEN
THE DOOR!

GAH!
AAAAARGH!
AAAAAAAAA
AAAAAAAAA
AAAAAAAAA
HHHHHHHHH!

just kidding.
it is not a monster.
it is the mailman.

oh.

oh.

don't be such a chicken.

Made in the USA
San Bernardino, CA
01 May 2018